This Book Belongs To:

_____

Read to Me Grandma

Stories, songs and rhymes for you to enjoy together

This is a Dempsey Parr Book
First published in 2000
Dempsey Parr is an imprint of Parragon
Parragon, Queen Street House, 4 Queen Street, Bath BA1 1HE, UK

Produced by The Templar Company plc,
Pippbrook Mill, London Road, Dorking, Surrey RH4 1JE, UK

Copyright © Parragon 2000

Compiled and edited by Caroline Repchuk
Designed by Kilnwood Graphics

Printed and bound in Spain
ISBN 1-84084-942-8

Read to Me Grandma

*Stories, songs and rhymes for
you to enjoy together*

DEMPSEY
PARR

Contents

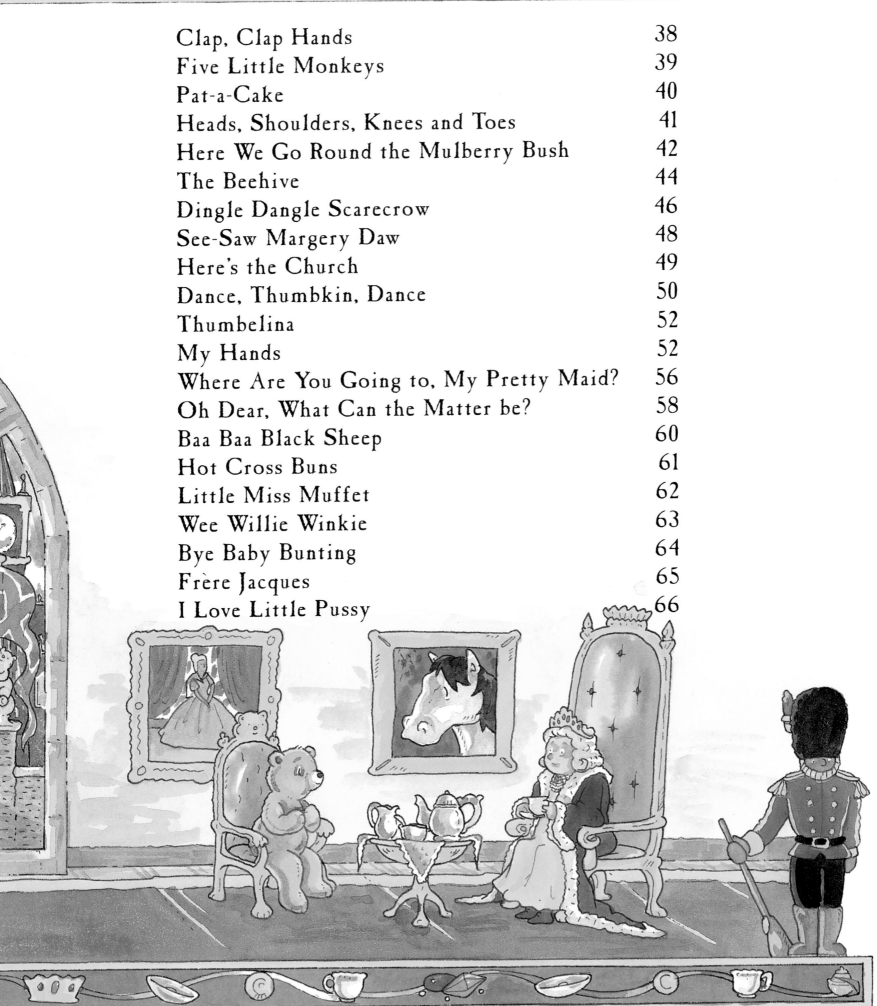

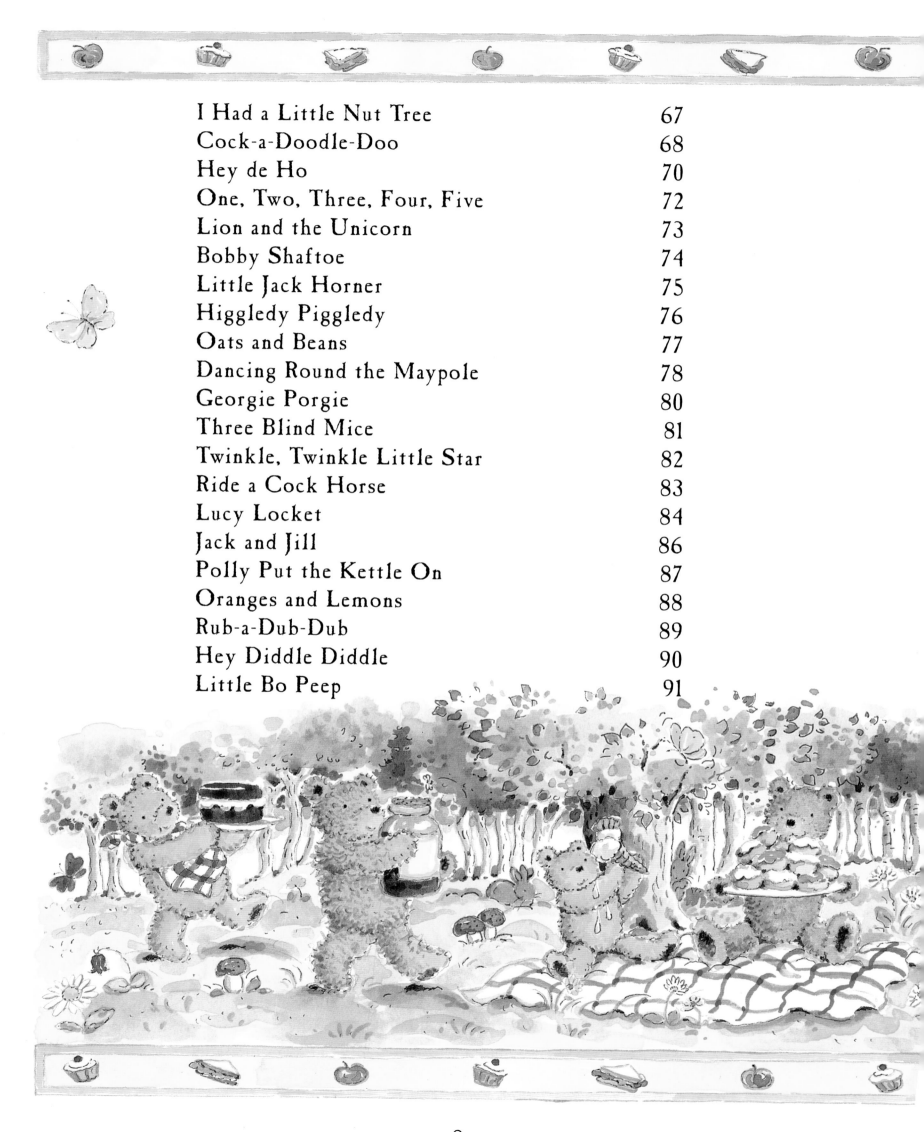

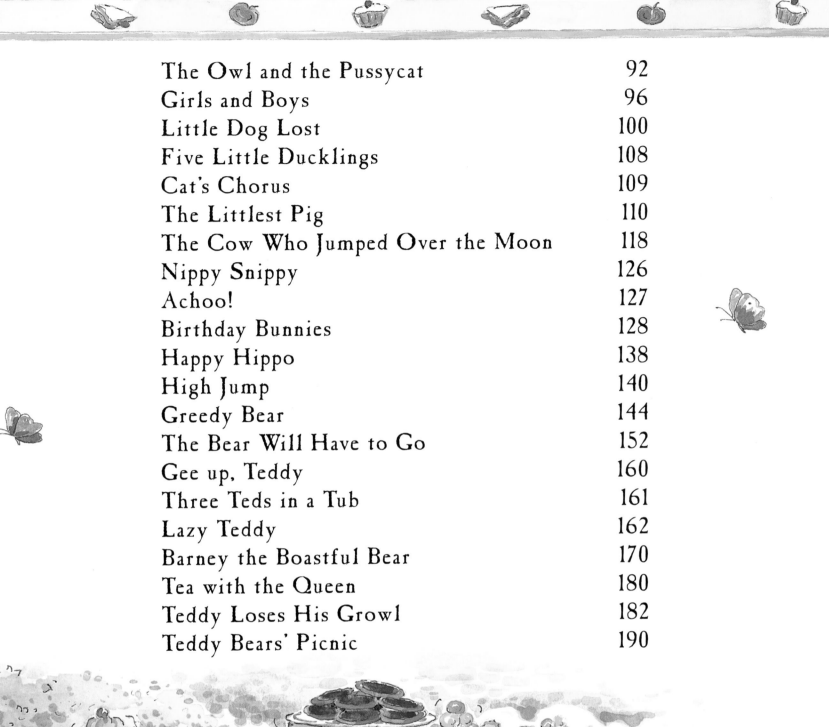

Action Songs

A collection of
traditional action
songs with easy
to follow pictures
to show you
what to do.

 # These Are Grandma's Glasses

These are Grandma's glasses,
This is Grandma's hat;
Grandma claps her hands like this,
And rests them in her lap.

Make rings round eyes

Mime hat with hands

Clap hands

Place hands in lap

These are Grandpa's glasses,
This is Grandpa's hat;
Grandpa folds his arms like this,
And has a little nap.

Make rings round eyes

Mime hat with hands

Fold arms

Pretend to sleep

Mousie

Make a fist and push other index finger in

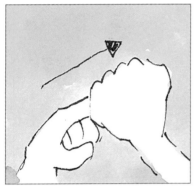

MOUSIE CREEPING

Push finger through until end appears

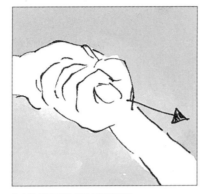

MOUSIE PEEPING

Wiggle finger

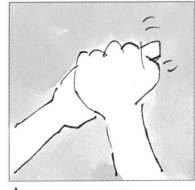

I'D LIKE TO STAY...

Pull finger back suddenly and hide!

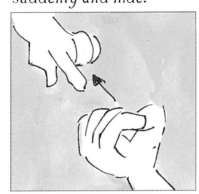

...POPS INTO HOLE

Mousie comes a-creeping, creeping.
Mousie comes a-peeping, peeping.
Mousie says, "I'd like to stay,
But I haven't time today."
Mousie pops into his hole
And says, "ACHOO!
I've caught a cold!"

Round and Round the Garden

Round and round
the garden,
Like a teddy bear;

One step, two step,
Tickle you under there!

Round and round
the haystack,
Went the little mouse.

One step, two steps,
In this little house.

Circle palm

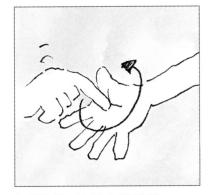

ROUND AND ROUND

Walk fingers up arm

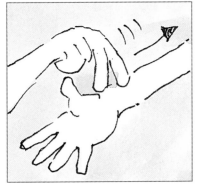

ONE STEP, TWO STEP

Tickle!

TICKLE!

Ring-A Ring-O'Roses

Ring-a-ring o'roses,
A pocket full of posies,
A-tishoo! A-tishoo!
We all fall down!

Dance around in a ring, pretend to sneeze, then fall down on the floor

Pop Goes the Weasel

Half a pound of tu'penny rice,
Half a pound of treacle.
That's the way the money goes,
POP! Goes the weasel.

A bouncing on the knee rhyme, with an extra big bounce on the "Pop!"

I'm a Little Teapot

SHORT

AND STOUT

HANDLE

SPOUT

I'm a little teapot
short and stout,
Here's my handle,
here's my spout,
When I get my
steam up hear me shout,
Tip me up
and pour me out.

STEAM UP

SHOUT

TIP

POUR

Okey Cokey

You put your left arm in, your left arm out,
In, out, in, out, you shake it all about,
You do the okey cokey, and you turn around,
And that's what it's all about.

Oh, the okey cokey,
Oh, the okey cokey,
Oh, the okey cokey,
Knees bend, arms stretch,
Ra, ra, ra!

*Rhyme continues with right arm, left leg,
right leg, whole self.*

LEFT ARM IN...

LEFT ARM OUT...

SHAKE IT ALL ABOUT...

TURN AROUND...

KNEES BEND, ARM STRETCH

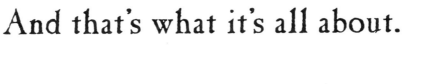

Turn Around

Turn around and touch the ground,
Turn around and touch the ground,
Turn around and touch the ground,
And fall right down.

The Baby in the Cradle

The baby in the cradle
Goes rock-a-rock-a-rock.

The clock on the dresser
Goes tick-a-tick-a-tock.

The rain on the window
Goes tap-a-tap-a-tap,

But here comes the sun,
So we clap-a-clap-a-clap!

Rock arms

ROCK

Swing arm side to side

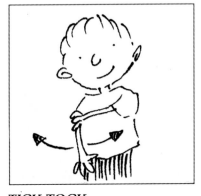

TICK-TOCK

Tap finger on hand

TAP-A-TAP

Clap!

CLAP

With My Hands on Myself

With my hands on myself,
what have we here?
This is my brainbox,
nothing to fear.
Brainbox and wibbly
wobbly woos,
That's what they taught me
when I went to school.

With my hands on myself,
what have we here?
These are my eye-peepers,
nothing to fear.
Eye-peepers, brainbox
and wibbly wobbly woos,
That's what they taught me
when I went to school.

With my hands on myself,
what have we here?
This is my nose-wiper,
nothing to fear.
Nose-wiper, eye-peepers,
brainbox and wibbly
wobbly woos,
That's what they taught me
when I went to school.

With my hands on myself,
what have we here?
This is my chest-protector,
nothing to fear.
Chest-protector, nose-wiper,
eye-peepers, brainbox and
wibbly wobbly woos,
That's what they taught me
when I went to school.

Wibbly woobly woos are the ear lobes, which should be wiggled whenever they are mentioned.
Additional verses could include bread basket (tummy), knee knockers (knees), and shoe stuffers (feet).

As Small as a Mouse

As small as a mouse,

As wide as a bridge,

As tall as a house,

As straight as a pin.

Slowly, Slowly

Slowly, slowly, very slowly
Creeps the garden snail.

Slowly, slowly, very slowly
Up the garden rail.

Quickly, quickly, very quickly
Runs the little mouse.

Quickly, quickly, very quickly
Round about the house.

Walk hand slowly up baby's tummy...

Tickle baby during second verse

If You're Happy and You Know It

If you're happy and you know it,
Clap your hands.
If you're happy and you know it,
Clap your hands.
If you're happy and you know it,
And you really want to show it,
If you're happy and you know it,
Clap your hands.

If you're happy and you know it,
Nod your head, etc.
If you're happy and you know it,
Stamp your feet, etc.

If you're happy and you know it,
Say "ha, ha!", etc.
If you're happy and you know it,
Do all four!

Five Little Peas

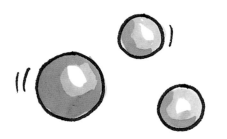

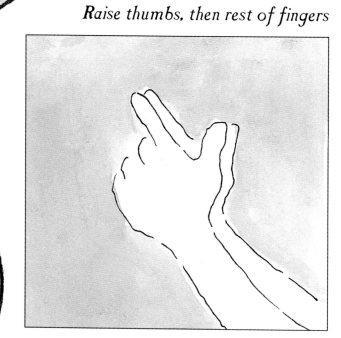

Clasp one hand around the other

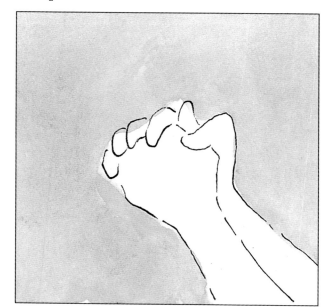

Five little peas in a pea-pod pressed,

Raise thumbs, then rest of fingers

One grew, two grew, and so did all the rest.

Move hands apart slowly

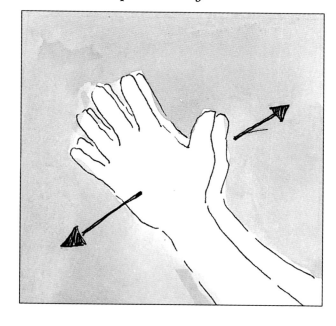

They grew, and they grew, and they did not stop,

Clap!

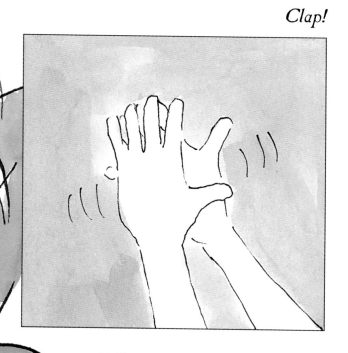

Until one day the pod went... POP!

One Finger, One Thumb

One finger, one thumb, keep moving,
One finger, one thumb, keep moving,
One finger, one thumb, keep moving,
We'll all be merry and bright.

One finger, one thumb,
one arm, keep moving,
One finger, one thumb,
one arm, keep moving,
One finger, one thumb,
one arm, keep moving,
We'll all be merry and bright.

One finger, one thumb, one arm,
one leg, keep moving, etc

One finger, one thumb,
one arm, one leg, one nod
of the head, keep moving, etc.

This rhyme may be continued with other verses - stand up, sit down, turn around, etc.

Incy Wincy Spider

Incy Wincy Spider climbing up the spout,
Down came the rain and washed the spider out.
Out came the sun, and dried up all the rain,
Incy Wincy Spider climbed up the spout again.

Touch opposite index fingers and thumbs together by twisting wrists

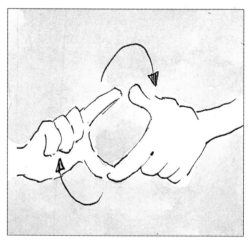

CLIMBING UP THE SPOUT...

Wiggle fingers as you lower them

DOWN CAME THE RAIN...

Make a big circle with arms. Repeat first action.

OUT CAME THE SUN...

The Ostrich

Here is the ostrich
straight and tall,

Nodding his head
above us all.

Here is the hedgehog
prickly and small,

Rolling himself
into a ball.

Hold up arm

Nod hand in air

Interlace fingers

Close hands in a ball

OSTRICH

NODS HIS HEAD

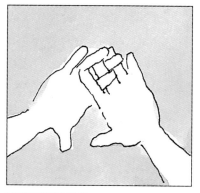

HEDGEHOG

HEDGEHOG IN BALL

Here is the spider scuttling around,
Treading so lightly on the ground.

Here are the birds that fly so high,
Spreading their wings across the sky.

Here are the children fast asleep,
And in the night the owls do peep,

"Tuit tuwhoo, tuit tuwhoo!"

Wriggle fingers

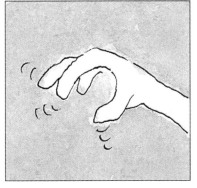

SPIDER

Lock thumbs together

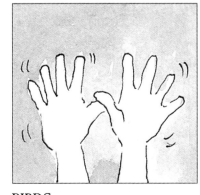

BIRDS

Pretend to sleep

CHILDREN ASLEEP

Make rings around eyes

OWLS

Scrub Your Dirty Face

Scrub your dirty face,
Scrub your dirty face,
With a rub-a-dub-dub,
And a rub-a-dub-dub,
Scrub your dirty face.

Mime actions. Continue with hands, knees and feet

Clap Your Hands

Clap your hands, clap your hands,
Clap them just like me.
Touch your shoulders, touch your shoulders,
Touch them just like me.
Tap your knees, tap your knees,
Tap them just like me.
Shake your head, shake your head,
Shake it just like me.
Clap your hands, clap your hands,
Then let them quiet be.

Jello on the Plate

Jello on the plate,
Jello on the plate,
Wibble, wobble,
Wibble, wobble,
Jello on the plate.

Rock from side to side

Bounce up and down

Candies in the jar,
Candies in the jar,
Shake them up,
Shake them up,
Candies in the jar.

Blow!

Candles on the cake,
Candles on the cake,
Blow them out,
Blow them out,
Puff, PUFF, PUFF!

Here's the Lady's Knives and Forks

Here's the lady's knives and forks.
Here's the lady's table.
Here's the lady's looking glass.
And here's the baby's cradle.
Rock! Rock! Rock! Rock!

Interlock fingers with backs of hands together

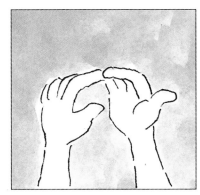

KNIVES AND FORKS...

Turn hands over and bring wrists together

TABLE...

Raise both index fingers

LOOKING GLASS...

Raise both little fingers and rock back and forth

CRADLE - ROCK!

Clap, Clap Hands

Clap, clap hands, one, two, three,
Put your hands upon your knees,
Lift them up high to touch the sky,
Clap, clap hands and away they fly.

Clap hands in rhythm   *Touch knees*   *Raise arms*   *Shake raised hands*

CLAP, CLAP HANDS   ...YOUR KNEES   ...LIFT THEM HIGH   ...AWAY THEY FLY

Five Little Monkeys

Five little monkeys jumping on the bed,
One fell off and bumped his head,
Mommy phoned the doctor and the doctor said,
"No more monkeys jumping on the bed!"

Four little monkeys...
Three little monkeys...
Two little monkeys...
One little monkey...

Repeat actions showing one less finger each time

Hold up hand	*Pat top of head*	*Pretend to hold phone*	*Waggle index finger*
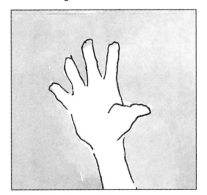			
FIVE LITTLE MONKEYS	...BUMPED HIS HEAD	...PHONED THE DOCTOR	NO MORE MONKEYS...

Pat-A-Cake

Pat-a-cake, pat-a-cake,
baker's man,

Bake me a cake,
as fast as you can.

Pat it and prick it and
mark it with B,

And put it in the oven
for Baby and me.

Clap in rhythm

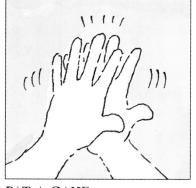

PAT-A-CAKE

Pat and 'prick' palm

PAT IT, PRICK IT

Trace the letter B on palm

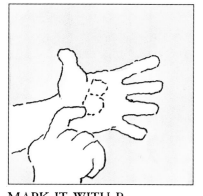

MARK IT WITH B

Put cake in oven

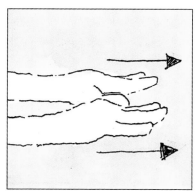

PUT IN THE OVEN

Head, Shoulders, Knees and Toes

Head, shoulders, knees
and toes, knees and toes,
Head, shoulders, knees
and toes, knees and toes,
And eyes and ears
and mouth and nose.
Head, shoulders, knees
and toes, knees and toes.

Sing slow at first, then faster.

Here We Go Round the Mulberry Bush

Here we go round the mulberry bush,
mulberry bush, mulberry bush,
Here we go round the mulberry bush,
on a cold and frosty morning.

This is the way we brush our hair,
brush our hair, brush our hair,
This is the way we brush our hair,
on a cold and frosty morning.

Repeat chorus

This is the way we clap our hands,
clap our hands, clap our hands,
This is the way we clap our hands,
on a cold and frosty morning.

Repeat chorus

This is the way we fall on the floor,
fall on the floor, fall on the floor,
This is the way we fall on the floor,
on a cold and frosty morning.

Repeat chorus

The Beehive

Here is the beehive.
Where are the bees?
Hidden away where nobody sees.
Soon they come
creeping out of the hive,
One, two, three, four, five!

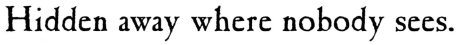

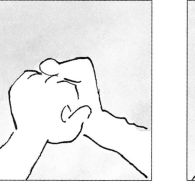

*Fold one hand over the
other to make hive*

Slowly bring out thumb...

*...followed by the other
fingers, one by one*

Suddenly tickle child!

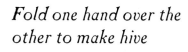
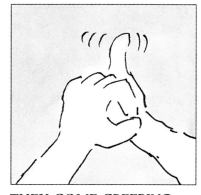

BEEHIVE

THEY COME CREEPING...

...THREE, FOUR...

...FIVE!

44

Dingle Dangle Scarecrow

When all the cows were sleeping
And the sun had gone to bed,
Up jumped the scarecrow
And this is what he said:

I'm a dingle dangle scarecrow
With a flippy floppy hat!
I can shake my arms like this,
I can shake my legs like that!

DINGLE DANGLE

FLIPPY FLOPPY HAT

When the cows were in the meadow
And the pigeons in the loft,
Up jumped the scarecrow
And whispered very soft:
Chorus

SHAKE MY ARMS

SHAKE MY LEGS

When all the hens were roosting
And the moon behind a cloud,
Up jumped the scarecrow
And shouted very loud:
Chorus

See-Saw, Margery Daw

See-Saw, Margery Daw,
Johnny shall have a new master,
He shall have but a penny a day,
Because he can't work any faster.

Rock backwards and forwards

48

Here Is the Church

Here is the church,

Here is the steeple,

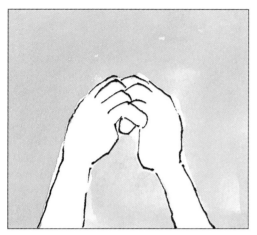

Interlace fingers

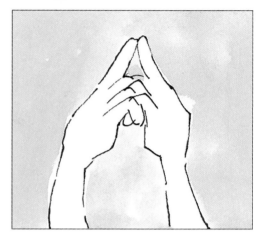

Point index fingers

Open the doors,

And here are the people.

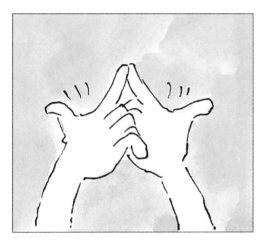

Open thumbs

Turn hands over and wiggle fingers

Here is the parson, going upstairs,

And here he is a-saying his prayers.

Walk fingers of one hand up fingers of other hand

Place palms together

49

Dance, Thumbkin, Dance

Make thumbs dance

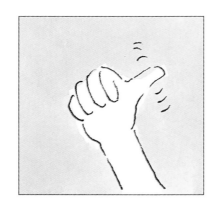

Dance, dance, thumbkin, dance.
Dance ye merrymen everyone.
Thumbkin he can dance alone,
He can dance alone.

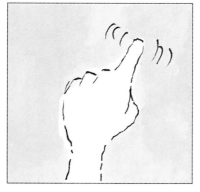

Dance, dance, foreman, dance.
Dance ye merrymen everyone.
Foreman he can dance alone,
He can dance alone.

Dance, dance, longman, dance.
Dance ye merrymen everyone.
Longman he can dance alone,
He can dance alone.

Dance, dance, ringman, dance.
Dance ye merrymen everyone.
Ringman he can dance alone,
He can dance alone.

Dance, dance, babyman, dance.
Dance ye merrymen everyone.
Babyman he can dance alone,
He can dance alone.

My Hands

My hands upon my head I place,
On my shoulders, on my face;
On my hips I place them so,
Then bend down to touch my toe.

Place hands on head   *...on shoulders*   *...on face*   *...on hips*

Now I raise them up so high,
Make my fingers fairly fly,
Now I clap them, one, two, three.
Then I fold them silently.

Touch toes

Raise hands in the air

Clap hands three times

Fold arms

Sing-Along Songs

A collection of traditional sing-along songs to enjoy together.

Where are you Going to My Pretty Maid?

Where are you going to, my pretty maid?
Where are you going to, my pretty maid?
I'm going a-milking, sir, she said,
Sir, she said, sir, she said,
I'm going a-milking, sir, she said.

May I go with you, my pretty maid?
May I go with you, my pretty maid?
You're kindly welcome, sir, she said,
Sir, she said, sir, she said,
You're kindly welcome, sir, she said.

What is your fortune, my pretty maid?

What is your fortune, my pretty maid?

My face is my fortune, sir, she said,

Sir, she said, sir, she said,

My face is my fortune, sir, she said.

Then I can't marry you, my pretty maid,

Then I can't marry you, my pretty maid,

Nobody asked you, sir, she said,

Sir, she said, sir, she said,

Nobody asked you, sir, she said.

Oh Dear, What Can The Matter Be?

Oh dear, what can the matter be?
Dear, dear, what can the matter be?
Oh dear, what can the matter be?
Johnny's so long at the fair.

He promised he'd buy me a basket of posies,
A garland of lilies, a garland of roses,
A little straw hat to set off the blue ribbons
That tie up my bonny brown hair.

Oh dear, what can the matter be?
Dear, dear, what can the matter be?
Oh dear, what can the matter be?
Johnny's so long at the fair.

Baa Baa Black Sheep

Baa, baa, black sheep,
Have you any wool?
Yes, sir, yes, sir,
Three bags full;
One for the master,
And one for the dame,
And one for the little boy
Who lives down the lane.

Hot Cross Buns!

Hot cross buns!

Hot cross buns!

One a-penny, two a-penny,

Hot cross buns!

If you have no daughters,

Give them to your sons,

One a-penny, two a-penny,

Hot cross buns!

Little Miss Muffet

Little Miss Muffet
Sat on a tuffet,
Eating her curds and whey;
There came a big spider,
Who sat down beside her,
And frightened Miss Muffet away.

Wee Willie Winkie

Wee Willie Winkie runs through the town,

Upstairs and downstairs in his nightgown,

Rapping at the windows, crying through the locks,

"Are the children in their beds,

It's past eight o'clock?"

Bye, Baby Bunting

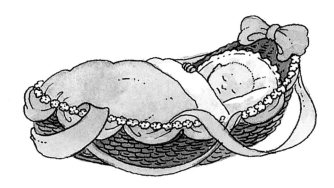

Bye, Baby Bunting

Daddy's gone a-hunting,

To find a little rabbit skin,

To wrap his Baby Bunting in.

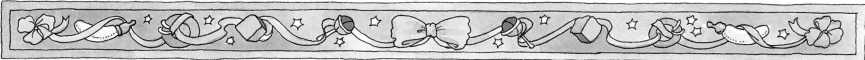

Frère Jacques

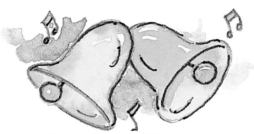

Frère Jacques, Frère Jacques,

Dormez-vous, dormez-vous?

Sonnez les matines, sonnez les matines,

Ding, dang, dong, ding, dang, dong.

I Love Little Pussy

I love little pussy,
her coat is so warm,
And if I don't hurt her
she'll do me no harm.
So I'll not pull her tail,
nor drive her away,
But Pussy and I very
gently will play.

I Had a Little Nut Tree

I had a little nut tree, nothing would it bear,

But a silver nutmeg and a golden pear;

The King of Spain's daughter came to visit me,

And all for the sake of my little nut tree.

I skipped over water, I danced over sea,

And all the birds in the air couldn't catch me.

Cock-a-Doodle-Doo

Cock-a-doodle-doo!

My dame has lost her shoe,

My master's lost his fiddling stick,

And doesn't know what to do.

Cock-a-doodle-doo!

What is my dame to do?

Till master finds his fiddling stick,

She'll dance without her shoe.

Cock-a-doodle-doo!

My dame has found her shoe,

And master's found his fiddling stick,

Sing cock-a-doodle-doo.

Hey de Ho

Hey de, hey de ho,
The great big elephant
Is so slow.
Hey de, hey de ho,
The elephant is so slow.

He swings his tail
From side to side,
As he takes the children
For a ride.

Hey de, hey de ho,
The elephant is so slow.

One, Two, Three, Four, Five

One, two, three, four, five,

Once I caught a fish alive.

Six, seven, eight, nine, ten,

Then I let him go again.

Why did you let him go?

Because he bit my finger so!

Which finger did he bite?

This little finger on the right.

The Lion and the Unicorn

The Lion and the Unicorn
Were fighting for the crown;
The Lion beat the Unicorn
All around the town.
Some gave them white bread,
And some gave them brown;
Some gave them plum cake,
And drummed them out of town.

Bobby Shaftoe

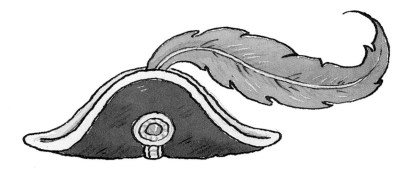

Bobby Shaftoe's gone to sea,
Silver buckles at his knee,
He'll come back and marry me,
Bonny Bobby Shaftoe.

Little Jack Horner

Little Jack Horner,

Sat in a corner,

Eating a Christmas pie.

He put in his thumb,

And pulled out a plum,

And said, "What a good boy am I!"

Higgledy-Piggledy

Higgledy-Piggledy,
My black hen,
She lays eggs for gentlemen;
Sometimes nine,
And sometimes ten,
Higgledy-Piggledy, my black hen!

Oats and Beans

Oats and beans and barley grow,
Oats and beans and barley grow,
Do you or I or anyone know,
How oats and beans and barley grow?

First the farmer sows his seeds,
Then he stands and takes his ease,
Stamps his feet and claps his hands,
Turns around to view the land.

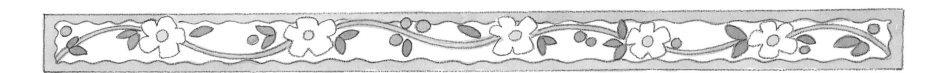

Dancing Round the Maypole

Dancing round the maypole,

Dancing all the day,

Dancing round the maypole,

On the first of May,

Dancing round the maypole,

What a merry bunch,

Dancing round the maypole,

Till it's time for lunch.

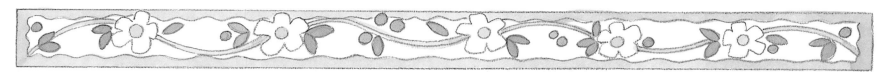

Dancing round the maypole,

Shouting out with glee,

Dancing round the maypole,

Till it's time for tea.

Dancing round the maypole,

Blue and white and red,

Dancing round the maypole,

Till it's time for bed.

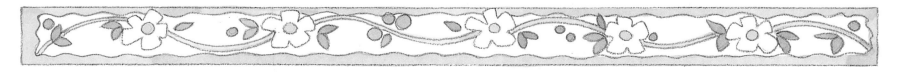

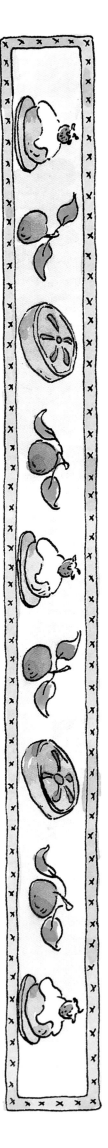

Georgie Porgie

Georgie Porgie, pudding and pie,
Kissed the girls and made them cry;
When the boys came out to play,
Georgie Porgie ran away.

Three Blind Mice

Three blind mice, three blind mice
See how they run, see how they run!
They all ran after the farmer's wife,
Who cut off their tails with a carving knife,
Did you ever see such a thing in your life,
As three blind mice?!

Twinkle, Twinkle, Little Star

Twinkle, twinkle, little star,
How I wonder what you are!
Up above the moon so high,
Like a diamond in the sky.

Ride A Cock-Horse

Ride a cock-horse to Banbury Cross,

To see a fine lady upon a white horse,

With rings on her fingers and bells on her toes

She shall have music wherever she goes.

Lucy Locket

Lucy Locket lost her pocket,
Kitty Fisher found it.
Not a penny was there in it,
Only ribbon round it.

Cinderella's umbrella's
Full of holes all over.
Every time it starts to rain
She has to run for cover.

Aladdin's lamp is getting damp,
And is no longer gleaming.
It doesn't spark within the dark,
But you can't stop it steaming.

Jack and Jill

Jack and Jill went up the hill
To fetch a pail of water;
Jack fell down and broke his crown
And Jill came tumbling after.

Up Jack got and home did trot
As fast as he could caper;
He went to bed to mend his head
With vinegar and brown paper.

Polly Put The Kettle On

Polly put the kettle on,
Polly put the kettle on,
Polly put the kettle on,
We'll all have tea.

Sukey take it off again,
Sukey take it off again,
Sukey take it off again,
They've all gone away.

Oranges and Lemons

Oranges and lemons,

Say the bells of St Clements.

I owe you five farthings,

Say the bells of St Martins.

When will you pay me?

Say the bells of Old Bailey.

When I grow rich,

Say the bells of Shoreditch.

Rub-A-Dub-Dub

Rub-a-dub-dub,

Three men in a tub,

And who do you think they be?

The butcher, the baker, the candlestick maker,

Turn them out knaves all three.

Hey Diddle, Diddle

Hey diddle, diddle,
The cat and the fiddle,
The cow jumped over the moon;
The little dog laughed to see such fun,
And the dish ran away with the spoon.

Little Bo Peep

Little Bo Peep has lost her sheep
And doesn't know where to find them;
Leave them alone, and they'll come home
Bringing their tails behind them.

The Owl and the Pussy-cat

The Owl and the Pussy-cat went to sea

In a beautiful pea-green boat,

They took some honey, and plenty of money,

Wrapped up in a five-pound note.

The Owl looked up to the stars above,

And sang to a small guitar,

"O lovely Pussy! O Pussy, my love,

What a beautiful Pussy you are,

You are, you are!

What a beautiful Pussy you are!"

Pussy said to the Owl, "You elegant fowl!

How charmingly sweet you sing!

"O let us be married! Too long we have tarried:

But what shall we do for a ring?"

They sailed away, for a year and a day,

To the land where the Bong-tree grows,

And there in a wood a Piggy-wig stood,

With a ring at the end of his nose,

His nose, his nose,

With a ring at the end of his nose.

"Dear Pig, are you willing to sell for one shilling
Your ring?" Said the Piggy, "I will."
So they took it away, and were married next day
By the Turkey who lives on the hill.

They dined on mince, and slices of quince,
Which they ate with a runcible spoon;
And hand in hand, on the edge of the sand,
They danced by the light of the moon,
The moon, the moon,
They danced by the light of the moon.

Girls and Boys

Girls and boys come out to play,

The moon doth shine as bright as day,

Leave your supper and leave your sleep,

And come with your playfellows into the street.

Come with a whoop, come with a call,

Come with a good will, or come not at all.

Up the ladder and down the wall,

A halfpenny bun will serve us all.

You find milk and I'll find flour,

And we'll have pudding in half an hour.

Animal Tales

Written by Caroline Repchuk

Entertaining
animal tales and
rhymes for you
to enjoy.

LITTLE DOG LOST

"Brrr," shivered Scruffy. "It's cold tonight."

"Well, snuggle up closer to me," said his mom.

"It's not fair," Scruffy grumbled. "Why do we have to sleep outside in the cold? The cats are allowed to sleep inside, in nice warm baskets!"

"We're farm dogs, dear," said Mom. "We have to be tough, and work hard to earn our keep."

"I'd rather be a cat," mumbled Scruffy. "All they do is wash themselves, eat and sleep."

"We don't have such a bad life," said Mom. "Now stop feeling sorry for yourself, and get some rest. We've got a lot of work to do tomorrow."

The next day, Scruffy woke early and trotted down the lane for a walk. He ran through the grass, chasing rabbits, and sniffing at the flowers.

Now, usually when he got to the end of the lane he stopped and turned back. But today, he saw a big red truck parked outside a house there. The back of the truck was open, and Scruffy thought he would just climb inside and take a look.

The truck was full of furniture. At the back was a big armchair with soft cushions. Scruffy clambered onto it. "I could doze all day, like a cat!" he told himself. He closed his eyes and before he knew it he had fallen fast asleep.

Scruffy awoke some time later with a sharp jolt.

"Oh, no, I fell asleep!" he groaned. "I'd better hurry back. We've got a busy day ahead!"

But then he saw that the truck doors were closed! He could hear voices outside.

"Oh, dear, I'll be in trouble if I get found in here," thought Scruffy, and he hid behind the chair.

The back of the truck opened and Scruffy peered out. Two men started unloading the furniture.

When Scruffy was sure that no one was looking, he crept out of the truck, but he was no longer in the countryside where he lived! He was in a big noisy town, full of buildings and cars.

Poor Scruffy had no idea where he was!

"The truck must have carried me away," thought Scruffy, feeling frightened.

All day long, Scruffy roamed around trying to find his way home, feeling cold, tired and hungry. At last, he lay down and began to howl miserably.

"What's the matter, pup?" he heard a man's kind voice say. "You look lost. Come home with me." Scruffy gave the man's hand a grateful lick, then jumped up and followed him home.

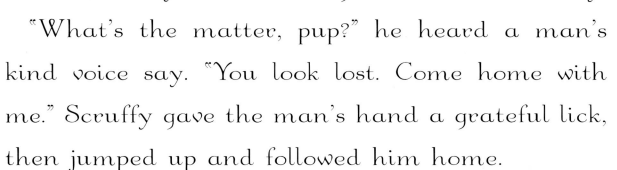

When they arrived at the man's house Scruffy sat on the doorstep, hoping the man might bring him some food out to eat. But the man said, "Come on in, you can't stay out there."

Scruffy followed the man in, and found a little poodle waiting to meet him. Scruffy stared at her in amazement. What had happened to her fur?

"You'd better take a bath before supper," said the man, looking at Scruffy's dirty white coat. The man washed him in a big tub, then brushed his tangled coat. Scruffy howled miserably. What had he done to deserve such punishment?

"Don't you like it?" asked the poodle, shyly.

"No, I don't," said Scruffy. "All this washing and cleaning is for cats!"

Next the man gave them supper — small bowls of dry pellets. Scruffy sniffed at them in disgust. He was used to chunks of meat and a nice big bone.

"This looks like cat food," said Scruffy, miserably.

After supper the poodle climbed into a big basket in the kitchen.

"I thought that belonged to a cat," said Scruffy. He tried sleeping in the basket but he was hot and uncomfortable. He missed counting the stars to help him fall asleep, and most of all he missed his mom.

"I want to go home," he cried, and big tears slipped down his nose.

The next day, the man put Scruffy on a lead and took him into town. He hated being dragged along, without being able to sniff at things.

Then, as they crossed the market place, Scruffy heard a familiar bark, and saw his mom's head hanging through the window of the farmer's truck! He started to howl, dragged the man over to where the truck was parked, then leapt up at the window barking excitedly. The farmer could hardly believe it was Scruffy — he had never seen him so clean! The man explained how he had found Scruffy, and the farmer thanked the man for taking such good care of him.

On the way back home, Scruffy told his mom all about his adventure and what had happened.

"I thought you had run away because you didn't like being a farm dog," she said gently.

"Oh, no, Mom," said Scruffy, quickly. "I love being a farm dog. I can't wait to get home to a nice big juicy bone and our little bed beneath the stars!"

FIVE LITTLE DUCKLINGS.

One, two, three, four, five,
Five little ducklings duck and dive,
Six, seven, eight, nine, ten,
Then swim home in a row again!

Why do they swim in rows?
The answer is nobody knows!
I wonder, as they swim past,
Who goes first and who goes last?

To the tune of 'Once I Caught A Fish Alive.'

CAT'S CHORUS

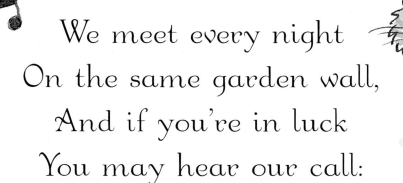

We meet every night
On the same garden wall,
And if you're in luck
You may hear our call:
With howl and a yowl, and a hullaballoo,
We're the cat's chorus, singing for you!

Fifi's soprano,
Butch sings the bass,
Kipper's a baritone,
Bert sets the pace.

Chorus

We sing lots of songs
Both new ones and old,
All huddled together
To keep out the cold.

Chorus

THE LITTLEST PIG

Little Pig had a secret. He snuggled down in the warm hay with his brothers and sisters, looked up at the dark sky twinkling with stars, and smiled a secret smile to himself. Maybe it wasn't so bad being the littlest pig after all...

Not so long ago, Little Pig had been feeling quite fed up. He was the youngest and by far the smallest pig in the family. He had five brothers and five sisters and they were all much bigger and fatter than he was. The farmer's wife called him Runt, as he was the smallest pig of the litter.

"I don't suppose little Runt will come to much," she told her friend Daisy, as they stopped by to bring the piglets some fresh hay.

His brothers and sisters teased him terribly. "Poor little Runtie," they said to him, giggling. "You must be the smallest pig in the world!"

"Leave me alone!" said Little Pig, and he crept off to the corner of the pig pen, where he curled into a ball, and started to cry. "If you weren't all so greedy, and let me have some food, maybe I'd be bigger!" he mumbled, sadly.

Every feeding time was the same — the others
all pushed and shoved, and shunted Little Pig
out of the way, until all that was left were the
scraps. He would never grow bigger at this rate.

Then one day Little Pig made an important
discovery. He was hiding in the corner of the pen,
as usual, when he spied a little hole in the fence
tucked away behind the feeding trough.

"I think I could fit through there!" thought Little Pig, excitedly.

He waited all day until it was time for bed, and then, when he was sure that all of his brothers and sisters were fast asleep, he wriggled through the hole. Suddenly he was outside, free to go wherever he pleased. And what an adventure he had!

First, he ran to the henhouse and gobbled up the bowls of grain. Then he ran to the field, slipped under the fence, and crunched up Donkey's carrots.

He ran into the vegetable patch and munched a whole row of cabbages. What a wonderful feast! Then, when his little belly was full to bursting, he headed for home. On the way he stopped by the hedgerow. What was that lovely smell? He rooted around until he found where it was coming from — it was a bank of wild strawberries.

Little Pig had never tasted anything so delicious. "Tomorrow night, I'll start with these!" he promised himself as he trotted back home to the pig pen.

Quietly he wriggled back through the hole, and soon fell fast asleep snuggled up to his mother, smiling contentedly.

Night after night Little Pig continued his tasty adventures, creeping out through the hole when the others were sleeping. He no longer minded when they pushed him out of the way at feeding time, as he knew a much better feast awaited him outside. Sometimes he would find the farm dog's bowl filled with scraps from the farmer's supper, or buckets of oats ready for the horses. "Yum, yum — piggy porridge!" he would giggle, as he gobbled it up.

But as the days and weeks went by, and Little Pig grew bigger and fatter, it was more of a squeeze to wriggle through the hole each night.

Little Pig knew that soon he would no longer be able to fit through the hole, but by then he would be big enough to stand up to his brothers and sisters. And for now he was enjoying his secret!

THE COW WHO
JUMPED OVER THE MOON

Boing, boing, boing! Bouncy Bunny kicked up her heels and bounded across the field.

"I can bounce high in the air, watch me!" she called to the other animals on the farm. Her fluffy white tail bobbed up and down.

"Very good!" said Silly Sheep, who was easily impressed.

"Yes, very good," said Swift, the sheepdog. "But not as good as me. I can jump right over the gate."

With that, he leapt over the gate and into the field.

"Amazing!" said Silly Sheep.

"Yes, amazing," said Harry Horse, with a flick of his mane. "But not as amazing as me. I can jump right over that hedge. Watch me!" And with that, he galloped around the field, then leapt high into the air, and sailed over the tall hedge.

"Unbelievable!" said Silly Sheep.

"Yes, unbelievable," said Daisy, the cow, chewing lazily on a clump of grass. "But not as unbelievable as me. I can jump right over the moon!"

"Well, I'm afraid that is unbelievable, Daisy," said Harry Horse. "No one can jump over the moon. That's just a fairy story."

"Well, I can," said Daisy, stubbornly. "And I can prove it! You can watch me do it if you like!"

The other animals all agreed that they would very much like to see Daisy jump over the moon.

"Meet me here in the field tonight, then," said Daisy to them. "When the moon is full, and the stars are shining bright."

So that night, when the moon had risen high up in the sky, the excited animals gathered together in the field. The rest of the animals from the farm came along too, for word had soon spread that Daisy the cow was going to jump over the moon, and they were all eager to watch.

"Come along then, Daisy," said Swift, the sheepdog, as the animals waited impatiently. "Are you going to show us how you can jump over the moon, or not?"

All the animals laughed, as they thought that Daisy was just boasting, and that she would not really be able to do it.

"Yes, I am going to show you," said Daisy, "but first of all, you will have to come with me. This isn't the right spot." Daisy led the animals across the field, to the far side, where a little stream ran along the edge of the field, separating it from the dark woods on the other side.

"Now, stand back everyone, and give me some room," said Daisy. The animals did as they were asked, and watched Daisy with anticipation, giggling nervously. Whatever was she going to do?

Daisy trotted back to the middle of the field, then ran towards the stream at a great speed.

At the last moment, she sprang into the air, and sailed across the stream, landing safely on the other side.

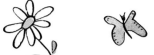

"I did it!" cried Daisy. "Aren't you going to clap, then?" The other animals looked at each other in confusion.

"But you only jumped over the stream!" said Harry Horse, puzzled.

"Come and take a closer look," called Daisy, still on the far side. The animals gathered close to

the water's edge. They looked down, and there reflected in the water shimmered the great full moon! How the animals laughed when they realized Daisy had tricked them.

"See?" said Daisy. "I really can jump over the moon!" And just to prove it, she jumped back to the field again. The animals all clapped and cheered.

"That was a very good trick!" said Swift.

"Amazing!" said Silly Sheep. "Could someone explain it to me again, please?"

NIPPY SNIPPY

Eeny, meeny, miney, mo,
Here comes Crab to pinch your toe!
Shout out loud and he'll let go -
Eeny, meeny, miney, mo!

Nippy, snippy, snappy, snip,
Be careful when you take a dip,
Or Crab will catch you in his grip!
Nippy, snippy, snappy, snip!

ACHOO!

Mouse's eyes filled up with water,
His little nose started to twitch,
A tingling tickled his whiskers,
And then his knees started to itch.

He got a bad case of the hiccups,
Then threw back his head in a sneeze,
And he said, "I'm most awfully sorry,
It's just I'm allergic to cheese!"

BIRTHDAY BUNNIES

"It's my first birthday tomorrow!" announced Snowy, a little white rabbit, very proudly. "Isn't that exciting?"

"Yes, very exciting!" said Whiskers, her brother. "Because it's my birthday too!"

"And mine!" said Patch.

"And mine!" said Nibble.

"And mine!" said Twitch.

"Do you think mom and dad have got a surprise for us?" asked Snowy.

"I hope so!" said Whiskers.

"Me too!" said Patch.

"Me too!" said Nibble.

"Me too!" said Twitch.

Mrs Rabbit was listening outside the door, as her children were getting ready for bed. She heard the little bunnies chattering excitedly about their birthdays the next day.

Whatever could she do to make it a special day for them? She sat and thought very hard, and later that evening, when Mr Rabbit came home, she said: "It is the childrens' first birthday tomorrow, and I'm planning a surprise for them. I want to make them a carrot cake, but I will need some carrots. Could you go and dig some nice fresh ones up from your vegetable garden?"

"Certainly, dear," said Mr Rabbit, and off he went back outside.

Mr Rabbit was proud of the carrots he grew.
They were very fine carrots, crunchy and sweet
and delicious. Every year he entered them in the
Country Show, and they nearly always won first
prize. So you can imagine his dismay when he
arrived at his vegetable patch to find that every
single carrot had been dug up and stolen!

He marched back inside. "Someone has stolen
my carrots!" he announced to his wife, crossly.
"And I am going to find out just who it is!"

And although it was getting late, he went back outside, and set off to find the naughty person.

First of all he stopped at Hungry Hare's house, and knocked at the door.

"Someone has stolen my carrots!" Mr Rabbit said. "Do you know who?"

"Oh, yes," said Hungry Hare. "But it wasn't me." And although Mr Rabbit pressed him, Hungry Hare would say no more.

Next Mr Rabbit went to Sly Fox's house.

"Someone has stolen my carrots!" he said. "Do you know who?"

"Oh, yes," said Sly Fox. "But it wasn't me." And although Mr Rabbit begged and pleaded with him, Sly Fox would say no more.

So Mr Rabbit marched to Bill Badger's house, and asked if he knew who had taken the carrots.

"Why, yes, in fact I do," said Bill Badger. "But it wasn't me."

And just like the others, he would say no more. It was the same wherever Mr Rabbit went, and although he got very cross, and stamped his foot, no one would tell him who had stolen his carrots!

"You'll find out soon enough," said Red Squirrel.

So Mr Rabbit went home feeling very puzzled.

"It seems that everyone knows who it was, but no one will tell me!" said Mr Rabbit to his wife.

"Not everyone, dear," she said. "I don't know who it was either. All I know is that it's our childrens' first birthday tomorrow, and we have no surprise for them." And feeling very miserable and confused, they went to bed, determined to get to the bottom of the mystery in the morning.

Next day the little bunnies came running into the kitchen, where their parents were having breakfast.

"Happy birthday, everyone!" called Snowy.

"Happy birthday!" cried the other little bunnies.

"Now, it's not much, but I wanted to give each of you a surprise!" Snowy went on. "By the way, I hope you don't mind, Dad." And with that Snowy pulled out a box of juicy carrots, each tied with a bow, and handed one to each of her brothers and sisters.

"Snap!" cried Whiskers, "I had just the same idea!" and he pulled out another box of carrots.

"Me too!" said Patch.

"Me too!" said Nibble.

"Me too!" said Twitch.

Soon there was a great pile of juicy carrots heaped on the kitchen table.

"So that's what happened to my carrots!" cried Mr Rabbit, in amazement. "I thought they had been stolen! And when he told the little bunnies the story they laughed till their sides ached. Then Mrs Rabbit put on her apron and shooed them outside.

"Just leave the carrots with me," she said.
"I have a birthday surprise of my own in store!"

And so the mystery was solved. It turned out
that Hungry Hare had seen the little bunnies
creep out one by one, and each dig up a few
carrots when they thought no one was looking.
He knew it was their birthdays and he guessed
what they were doing. He had told the other forest
folk, and everyone thought it was a great joke.

Mr Rabbit felt very ashamed that he had been so cross with everyone, when they were really just keeping the secret. To apologise, he invited them for a special birthday tea that afternoon, which the little bunnies thought was a great surprise.

And of course the highlight of the day was when Mrs Rabbit appeared from the kitchen carrying, what else, but an enormous carrot cake!

HAPPY HIPPOPOTAMUS

Hey! look at me,
A happy hippopotamus,
Covered with mud
From my head to my bottom-us!
Squishing and squelching
And making an awful fuss,
Rolling around in my bath!

I like to blow bubbles
Breath out through my nose-es,
To wriggle and jiggle
The mud through my toes-es,
And would you believe it
That I smell like roses,
When I come out of my bath!

To the tune of 'Oh, dear, what can the matter be?'

HIGH JUMP

The Shrew said to the Kangaroo,
"I can jump as high as you!"
Laughed Kanga, "How can that be true
Of one so small, please tell me, do!"

Said Shrew, "I'll show you, then you'll see,
I'll jump so high, I'll reach that tree!
But first of all you must agree,
To show your jumping skills to me!"

Then Kanga bounced into the air,
So busy he was unaware
That Shrew was clinging to his hair
To reach the treetop – most unfair!

Back Kanga landed on the ground,
"Your turn," he said, and spun around.
"Up here!" called Shrew, a distant sound.
"Well," said Kanga, "I'll be bound!"

Teddy Tales

Written by Caroline Repchuk, Claire Keen and Andrew Charman

A teddy tale for
everyone,
and some
teddy rhymes
too!

GREEDY BEAR

If there is one thing in the whole wide world that a teddy bear likes more than anything it is buns — big sticky cinnamon buns with sugary tops, and squishy middles. A teddy bear will do almost anything for a bun. But for one greedy little teddy bear called Clarence, sticky buns were to be his unsticking!

Rag Doll baked the most wonderful buns in the little toy cooker. She baked big buns and small buns, iced buns and cinnamon buns, raisin buns and poppy-seed buns, and even hot-cross buns! She shared them out amongst the toys in the playroom, and everybody loved them. But no-one loved them as much as Clarence.

"If you will give me your bun, I'll polish your boots!" he'd say to Tin Soldier.

And sometimes if Tin Soldier was not feeling too hungry, he'd agree. There was always someone who would give Clarence their bun in return for a favor, and sometimes Clarence would eat five or six buns in one day!

Then he'd be busy washing the dolls' dresses, brushing Scotty Dog's fur, or cleaning the toy policeman's car. He would even stand still and let the clown throw custard pies at him!

So you see, Clarence was not a lazy bear, but he was a greedy bear, and in spite of all his busyness, he was becoming a rather plump little greedy bear. All those buns were starting to show around his middle, and his fur was beginning to strain at the seams!

Then one day Clarence rushed into the playroom full of excitement. His owner, Penny, had told him that next week she was taking him on a teddy bears' picnic.

"She says there will be honey sandwiches and

ice-cream and cookies – and lots and lots of buns!"
Clarence told the others, rubbing his hands
together. "I can hardly wait! In fact all this
excitement has made me hungry, so I think I'll
have a bun." And he took a big sticky bun out
from under a cushion where he'd hidden it earlier.

"Oh, Clarence!" said Rabbit. "One of these days
you will simply go pop!"

"Just be happy I don't like carrots!" said
Clarence with a smile.

Well, that week Clarence was busier than ever. Every time he thought about the picnic it made him feel hungry, and then he'd have to find someone who'd let him have their bun. He ate bun after bun, and would not listen when Rag Doll warned him that his back seam was starting to come undone.

The day of the teddy bears' picnic dawned, and Clarence yawned and stretched, smiling to himself with excitement. But as he stretched he felt a strange popping sensation all down his stomach. He tried to sit up in bed, but to his alarm he found he could not move. He looked down to see that the seams around his tummy had popped open, and his stuffing was spilling out all over the bed!

"Help!" he cried. "I'm exploding!"

Just then, Penny woke up. "Oh, Clarence!" she cried when she saw him. "I can't take you to the teddy bears' picnic like that!"

Penny showed Clarence to her mommy, who said he would have to go to the toy hospital.

Clarence was away from the playroom for a whole week, but when he came back he was as good as new. Some of his stuffing had been taken out, and he was all sewn up again.

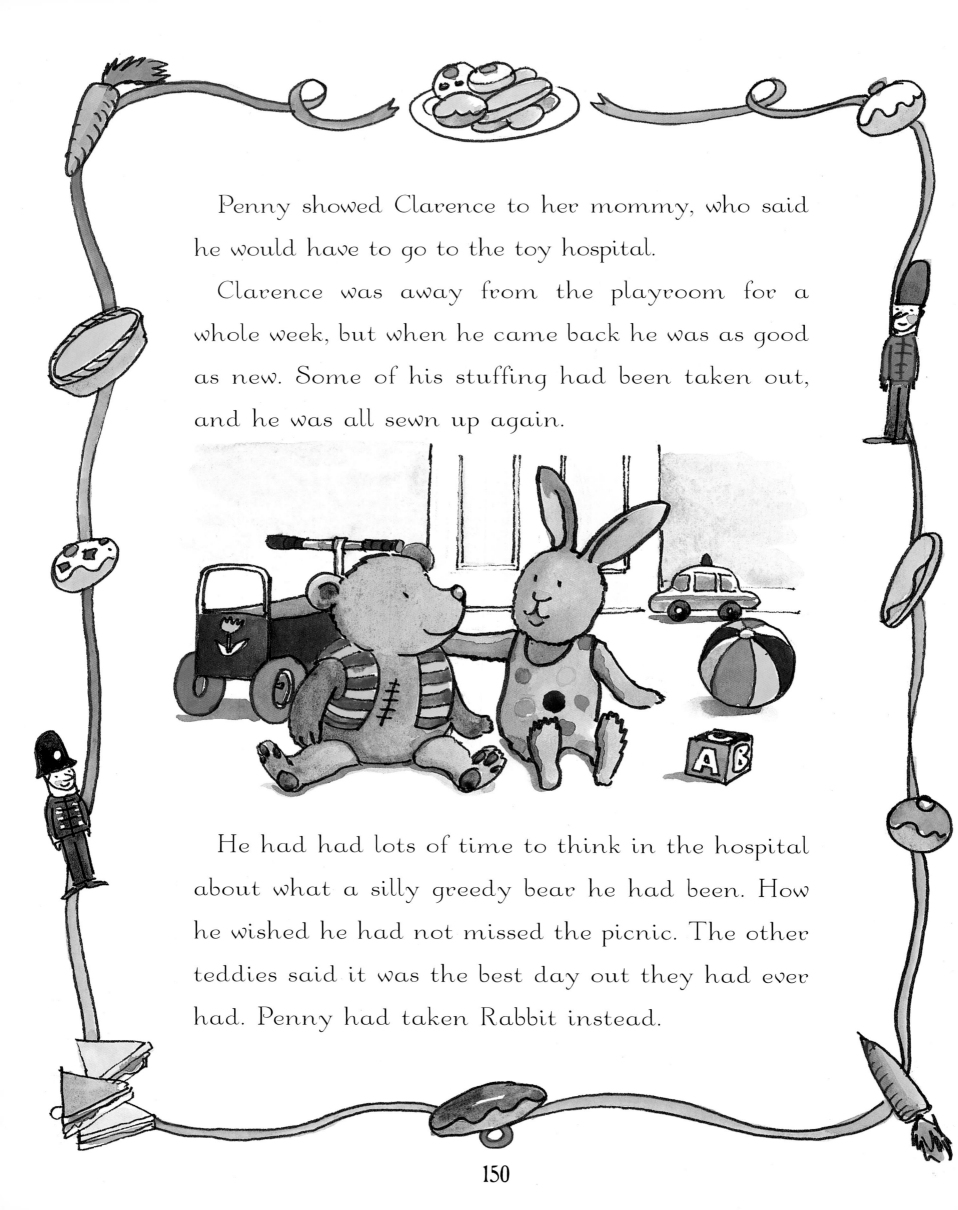

He had had lots of time to think in the hospital about what a silly greedy bear he had been. How he wished he had not missed the picnic. The other teddies said it was the best day out they had ever had. Penny had taken Rabbit instead.

"It was terrible," moaned Rabbit. "Not a carrot in sight. I did save you a bun though." And he pulled a big sticky bun out of his pocket.

"No thank you, Rabbit," said Clarence. "Funnily enough, I've gone off buns!"

Of course, Clarence did not stop eating buns for long, but from then on he stuck to one a day. And he still did favors for the others, only now he did them for free!

151

THE BEAR
WILL HAVE TO GO

While Lucy slept in the shade of a tree, Cuthbert went for a walk into the woods and was soon quite lost. He had no idea which way was back, so he sat down and thought about what to do next.

When Lucy awoke, she looked around in surprise. Her teddy bear, Cuthbert, was missing. She thought someone had taken him, for she didn't know that when people are asleep their teddy bears like to go walking.

"Cuthbert!" she called. "Cuthbert, where are you?"

He wasn't very far away. Lucy soon found him sniffing at a clump of moss.

"There you are!" she sighed. "I thought I'd lost you. Where's your waistcoat?"

In fact, Lucy really had lost Cuthbert, for the bear she was now taking home was not a teddy bear at all, but a real baby bear cub! As they ran back through the woods, the bear in Lucy's arms kept very still. He stared straight ahead without blinking, and tried not to sneeze. Soon they were back in Lucy's bedroom. Lucy flung the bear on her bed, then went to run a bath.

"Time to escape!" thought the bear. He slid off the bed, pulling the covers after him. He ran over to the window and tried to climb up the curtains. They tore down and tumbled to a heap on the floor. Just then Lucy's mother came into the room. The bear froze. Then Lucy appeared.

"Look at this mess," said Lucy's mother. "You've been playing with that bear again. Please tidy up."

Lucy had no idea how her room had got in such a mess, but she tidied up, took the bear into the bathroom and put him on the edge of the tub.

"Don't fall in," she said, and went to fetch a towel. The bear jumped into the tub with a great splash. He waved his paws wildly sending sprays of soapy water across the room. When he heard footsteps, he froze and floated on his back in the water as if nothing was wrong. It was Lucy, followed by her mother. "Oh, Lucy! What a mess!"

"Cuthbert must have fallen in," cried Lucy, rubbing his wet fur with a towel.

"A teddy bear couldn't make all this mess on its own," said Lucy's mother. "Please clean it up."

Lucy looked carefully at Cuthbert. Something was different about him, but she just couldn't work out what it was.

That night, while Lucy slept, the bear tip-toed downstairs. He needed to get back to the woods where he belonged, but he was hungry. In the kitchen he found lots of food, and he had a feast.

When Lucy came down for a glass of milk she found him with food all over his paws. The bear froze. Then her mother appeared in the doorway.

"This is the last straw, Lucy," said her mother, crossly. "You have been very naughty today, and every time something happens you've got that bear with you. If there is any more bad behaviour, the bear will have to go."

When her mother had gone back upstairs, Lucy looked carefully at the bear.

"You're not Cuthbert are you?" she said. The bear looked back at her and blinked. Lucy gasped. "You're a real bear!"

Now all the mess made sense! Lucy could hardly believe she had made such a mistake. She stroked the bear gently and he licked her finger.

"I'd better get you back to the woods before there's any more trouble," she said. "And I'd better try to find the real Cuthbert."

So early next morning, before her parents were awake, she crept out of the house carrying the bear. Out in the woods she put the bear on the ground. He licked her hand and padded away.

Lucy was sad to see the little bear go. She wiped a tear from her eye as she turned away... and there at the foot of a tree sat her teddy bear, Cuthbert! Lucy picked him up and hugged him.

"Where have you been?" she asked. "You'll never guess the trouble I've been in. What have you been doing all night?"

Cuthbert said nothing. He just smiled. What had he been doing all night? Well, that's another story!

GEE UP, TEDDY

Gee up, Teddy,
Don't you stop!
Ride on the
hobbyhorse,
Clippety clop!
Clippety clopping,
Round and round.
Giddy up,
We're toybox bound!

THREE TEDS IN A TUB

Rub-a-dub, dub,
Three teds in a tub,
Sailing across the sea!
But the rumble of tums,
And the smell of hot buns,
Will bring them back home for tea!

LAZY TEDDY

There was nothing Lazy Teddy liked more than to be tucked up snug and warm in Joshua's bed. Every morning the alarm clock would ring and Joshua would leap out of bed and fling open the curtains. "I love mornings!" he'd say, stretching his arms up high as the sun poured in through the window. "You're crazy!" Teddy would mutter, and he'd burrow down beneath the quilt to the bottom of the bed, where he'd spend the rest of the morning snoozing happily.

"Come out and play, you lazy bear," Joshua would call. But Lazy Teddy wouldn't budge. He would just snore even louder.

Joshua wished that Teddy would be more lively, like his other friends' bears. He loved having adventures, but they would be even better if Teddy would share them with him.

One evening, Joshua decided to have a talk with Teddy before they went to bed. He told him all about the fishing trip he'd been on that day with his friends and their teddy bears.

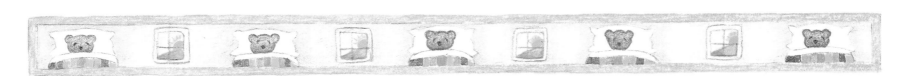

"It was lots of fun, Teddy. I wish you'd been there. It really is time you stopped being such a lazybones. Tomorrow is my birthday, and I'm having a party. There will be games, and presents and ice-cream. Please promise you'll come?"

"It does sound like fun," said Teddy. "Okay, I promise. I'll get up just this once."

The next morning, Joshua was up bright and early. "Yippee, it's my birthday today!" he yelled, dancing round the room. He pulled the covers off his bed. "Come on, Teddy, time to get up!"

"Just five more minutes!" groaned Teddy, and he rolled over and fell straight back to sleep. When Joshua came back up to his room after breakfast, Teddy still wasn't up. Well, by now Joshua was getting quite cross with Teddy. He reached over and poked him in the tummy. Teddy opened one eye and growled. "Wake up, Teddy! You promised, remember?" said Joshua.

Teddy yawned. "Oh, if I must!" he said, and muttering and grumbling he climbed out of bed. He washed his face and paws, brushed his teeth and put on his best red vest.

"There, I'm ready!" he said.

"Good," said Joshua. "About time too!"

Just then the doorbell rang, and Joshua ran to answer it. "I'll come and fetch you in a minute," he said to Teddy. But when he returned there was no sign of Teddy, just a gentle snoring coming from the bottom of the bed.

Joshua was so cross and upset with Lazy Teddy, that he decided to leave him right where he was.

"He'll just have to miss the party!" he said. Deep down though, he was hurt that Teddy wouldn't keep his promise.

Joshua enjoyed his party, although he wished that Teddy had been there. That night when he got into bed, he lay crying quietly into his pillow.

Teddy lay awake in the dark, listening. He knew Joshua was crying because he had let him down, and he felt very ashamed of himself.

"I'm sorry!" whispered Lazy Teddy, and he snuggled up to Joshua and stroked him with a paw until he fell asleep.

The next morning when the alarm clock rang, Joshua leapt out of bed, as usual. But what was this? Teddy had leapt out of bed too, and was stretching his paws up high. Joshua looked at him in amazement.

"What are we doing today, then?" asked Teddy.

"G...g...going for a picnic," stammered Joshua, in surprise. "Are you coming?"

"Of course," said Teddy. And from that day on, Teddy was up bright and early every day, ready to enjoy another day of adventures with Joshua, and he never let him down again.

BARNEY THE BOASTFUL BEAR

Barney was a very boastful bear.

"Look at my lovely soft fur!" he would say to the other toys. "See how it shines!"

Barney loved to talk about himself. "I'm the smartest toy in the playroom!" he would say. "It's a well-known fact."

He didn't know that the other toys all laughed about him behind his back.

"That bear thinks he's so smart," growled Scotty Dog. "But he isn't smart enough to know when everyone's fed up with him!"

"He'll learn his lesson one of these days," said Molly Monkey, and sure enough, that is just what happened...

One hot summer's day, the toys lazed in the warm playroom. "Wouldn't it be lovely if we could go for a walk outside," said Rag Doll.

"We could have a lovely picnic in the woods!" said Old Bear.

"Even better, we could go for a drive in the toy car first!" said Rabbit.

"But none of us is big or clever enough to drive the toy car," said Rag Doll, sadly.

"I am!" came a voice from the corner. It was Barney. He had been listening to them talking.

"I can drive the toy car. And I know the best place for a picnic in the woods," he said.

"We've never seen you drive the car," said Rabbit, suspiciously.

"That's because I drive it at night, when you're asleep," said Barney. "I'm a very good driver, in fact."

"Ooh, let's go then!" cried Rag Doll. And in no time they had packed up a picnic and were sitting ready in the car.

"Er, I don't feel like driving today, actually," mumbled Barney. "It's too hot." But the others were not interested in hearing excuses, so rather reluctantly Barney climbed into the driver's seat and started the engine. You see, the truth was, Barney had never really driven the car before, and he was scared. But he wanted to show off, so he pretended to know what he was doing.

Off they set down the garden path. "Toot, toot!" Barney beeped the horn as he turned the little car out into the country lane, and soon they were driving along, singing merrily.

All was going well, until Rag Doll suddenly said, "Hey, Barney, didn't we just miss the turning for the woods?"

"I know where I'm going," said Barney, crossly. "Leave it to me." And he made the little car go faster.

"Slow down a bit, Barney!" called Old Bear, from the back seat. "My fur is getting all ruffled." He was starting to feel anxious.

"I don't need a back seat driver, thank you," said Barney, with a growl, and made the car go even faster. By now the others were starting to feel scared, but Barney was having a great time.

"Aren't I a wonderful driver!" he chuckled. "Look – no hands!" And he took his paws off the steering wheel. Just then they reached a sharp corner. The little car went spinning off the side of the road and crashed into a tree, tipping all the toys out into the ditch!

They were a bit dazed, but luckily no one was hurt. They were not pleased with Barney though. "You silly bear!" said Rabbit, crossly. "We could have all been badly hurt!"

"We'll have to walk home now," said Rag Doll, rubbing her head. "Where are we?"

Everyone looked at Barney.

"Don't ask me!" he said, quietly.

"But you said you knew the way!" said Old Bear, indignantly.

"I was only pretending," said Barney, his voice trembling. "I don't really know how to drive, and I don't know where we are!" And he started to cry.

The other toys were furious with Barney.

"You naughty boastful bear!" they scolded. "Now see what trouble your boasting has got us into!"

The lost toys walked through the dark woods all night long, clinging together in fright as shadows loomed around them.

They had never been out at night before. Then just before dawn, they spotted the little house where they lived, and crept back into the playroom.

What a relief it was to be home again!
Luckily their owner had not noticed they
were missing, so she never knew what an
adventure her toys had been having while
she was fast asleep. She often wondered what
had happened to her toy car though.

As for Barney, he was very sorry for the
trouble he had caused. After a while the other
toys forgave him, and from that day on he never
boasted about anything again.

TEA WITH THE QUEEN

Teddy bear, teddy bear,
Where have you been?
I've been up to London to visit the queen!

I went to her palace,
And knocked at the gate,
And one of her soldiers said, please would I wait?

Then one of her footmen,
All dressed in red,
Led me inside, saying, step this way, Ted!

And there in a huge room,
High on her throne,
Sat the poor queen, taking tea all alone.

She said, how delightful,
Sit down, fill your tum!
And soon we were chattering just like old chums!

And when time came to leave,
She shook hands and then,
She said, come back soon, we must do it again!

TOUGH TED LOSES HIS GROWL

The alarm clock started to ring and Katie jumped out of bed, bursting with energy. Tough Ted opened one sleepy eye (which was all he could do, as the other one had fallen off years ago) and stretched.

"Another morning," he yawned. "I don't suppose it will be a good one."

Tough Ted was a very old bear. He had belonged to Katie's mom when she was young. He had been a smart teddy then, and happy, but now he was in a sorry state and was always grumpy. He was the oldest of the toys and he had been through some tough times. The other toys loved him, but they were fed up with his constant moaning and groaning.

"When is this bed going to be made? I can't get comfortable with all these covers thrown back!" he complained. "And they should pull that blind down, the sun's shining straight into my eye," he grumbled.

"Talking of which, it's about time they gave me a new one," he moaned. He carried on growling all morning.

"If he doesn't stop complaining soon I'm going to stuff my hat in his mouth," whispered Soldier to Clown, as they sat on the shelf.

"Not if I put my juggling balls in there first!" said Clown. All the toys giggled.

"It's about time we taught him a lesson," said Rag Doll. "What can we do to stop him moaning?"

"What about sticking a band-aid over his mouth while he's asleep?" twittered Owl, who was always wise.

"That's a brilliant idea, Owl!" said Rag Doll, and everyone agreed.

So that night, Rag Doll fetched a band-aid from the bathroom cabinet, and stuck it firmly over Tough Ted's mouth while he was asleep. All the toys were delighted – peace and quiet at last!

The next morning the alarm went off and Katie went into the bathroom. Tough Ted opened his eye and was just about to moan that the alarm was still ringing, when he realized he could not open his mouth!

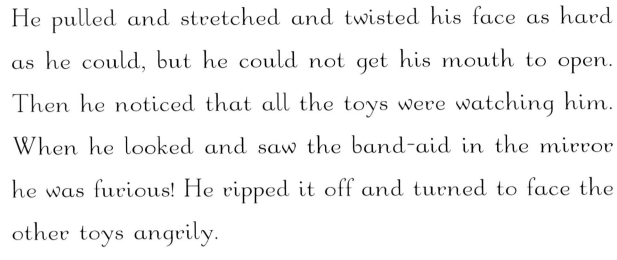

He pulled and stretched and twisted his face as hard as he could, but he could not get his mouth to open. Then he noticed that all the toys were watching him. When he looked and saw the band-aid in the mirror he was furious! He ripped it off and turned to face the other toys angrily.

"Who did this?" he bellowed. "When I find out who it was, there'll be trouble, growwwll! Have you no respect for an old bear?" He went on and on and on. He grew red in the face, and looked terribly cross. All the toys became quite scared.

Then, as he was growling at the top of his voice, a funny thing happened. His voice began to crack. He tried to clear his throat, but it was no use. He had lost his voice completely!

"Well it serves you right!" said Rag Doll. "All you do is moan, moan, moan, and we're tired of listening to you. We put the band-aid on your mouth to teach you a lesson. But now you've moaned so much that you've made yourself lose your voice completely."

With that a big tear rolled down Tough Ted's cheek. He was not so tough after all. He had not realised that he moaned so much, and he felt very sorry.

Rag Doll did not like seeing Tough Ted so sad. All the toys felt a bit guilty for what they had done.

"I'll go and get you some honey from the kitchen," said Rag Doll. "It will soothe your throat. But you must promise not to start moaning again."

After Rag Doll had given Tough Ted a spoonful of honey, he whispered, "I'm sorry. I promise I'll try not to moan any more. I didn't realise I'd become such a grumpy old bear."

With that, all the toys gave Tough Ted a hug and Rag Doll gave him some more honey.

Since then Tough Ted has tried really hard not to moan. But whenever he does, he thinks about the band-aid and quickly stops himself before anyone hears! And the rest of the toys do their best to look after him and keep him happy.

TEDDY BEARS' PICNIC

Little Bear brought chocolate cake,
Raggy Bear brought honey,
Baby Bear brought ice-cream,
With butterscotch all runny!

Tough Old Ted brought cinnamon buns,
Silky Bear brought jello,
Shaggy Bear brought cookies and
Egg sandwiches all yellow!

Woolly Bear brought pecan pie,
Tiny Ted brought candy,
Mrs Bear brought little plates
She thought would come in handy.

Off they set into the woods,
A sunny spot they found,
And had a teddies picnic,
As they shared the goodies round!

Illustrations by:
Georgie Birkett, Stephanie Boey, Mario Capaldi,
Dorothy Clark, Kate Davies, Maggie Downer, Frank Endersby,
Serena Feneziani, Andrew Geeson, Piers Harper, Elaine Keary,
Angela Kincaid, Jane Molineaux, Claire Mumford, Rikki O'Neill,
Pauline Siewart, Jessica Stockham and Linda Worrell.